CHARLOTTE ZOLOTOW
pictures by Kathryn Jacobi

Who Is Ben?

HarperCollins*Publishers*

Who Is Ben?
Text copyright © 1997 by Charlotte Zolotow
Illustrations copyright © 1997 by Kathryn Jacobi
Printed in the U.S.A. All rights reserved.

Library of Congress Cataloging-in-Publication Data
Zolotow, Charlotte, date
    Who is Ben? / by Charlotte Zolotow ; pictures by Kathryn Jacobi.
        p.   cm.
    Summary: On a moonless, starless night, a young boy feels at one
with the darkness, thinking about where he came from before he was
born and where he will go after he dies.
    ISBN 0-06-027351-8. — ISBN 0-06-027352-6 (lib. bdg.)
    [1. Identity—Fiction.   2. Night—Fiction.]   I. Jacobi, Kathy, ill.   II. Title.
PZ7.Z77Whf   1997   96-2382
[E]—dc20   CIP
                                                                      AC

Typography by Tom Starace
1   2   3   4   5   6   7   8   9   10
❖
First Edition

It was a very black night.
No moon. No stars.

But inside Ben's house it was warm and cozy.

He didn't turn on the light
when he went upstairs
to his room.

He crossed in the darkness
and looked out the window
He couldn't see the house
across the street.
He couldn't see the front steps
of his own house.
He couldn't see the giant copper beech tree
that grew in their yard.
Just blackness.
Everything black.
It was as though
there were nothing in the world.

He couldn't see himself,
he was part of the indoor blackness,
which was part of the outdoor blackness.
It was a strange secret feeling.
He felt that he was all there was.
He felt he was not really here.
He was really the blackness itself,
smooth and velvety and dark and safe,
he was blended with the black night
with no moon.
No stars. No copper beech. No front steps.

No one else in the world,
just the big enfolding dark
that was part of him,
and he was part of it,
as though in this quiet darkness
he was the moon and the stars
and the copper beech.

Just then his mother came in the room
and turned on the light.
The room around him
was warm and cozy,
the bed turned down,
and the bureau and desk and chair
looked bright and exciting as though
he had never seen them before.

"Why are you in the dark?" his mother said.
But instead of answering
he surprised them both.
"Where was I before I was born?" he asked.
But he felt the answer,
he had been part of that strange
trembling huge blackness
with no light and no sound,
no beginning and no end.

And where will I be when I die?
But again he felt the answer,

no moon, no stars,
no beginning
no end
he was it
and it was Ben.